The Sea of Adventure

Dinah peered in through a dirty and cracked window. The hut was dark and empty inside.

"There's no one there," she said.

"Let's go in," decided Philip, and opened the door. "We've got to get out of this storm."

The children all trooped inside. Jack struck a match and they checked out their new shelter.

Suddenly Lucy-Ann screamed. They turned and looked in the direction in which she was pointing.

Staring at them through the window was a wild and frightening face. Big bulging eyes glared in a face lined with elaborate designs and decorations. The face bared its teeth at them in a grimace, then moved over to the door. The handle turned and the door began to open . . .

*There are eight screenplay novelisations
starring Philip, Dinah, Jack and Lucy-Ann from the
Channel Five Enid Blyton™ Adventure Series:*

*All published by
HarperCollinsPublishers Ltd*

Enid Blyton's™

The Sea of
Adventure

Screenplay novelisation by
Nigel Robinson

Collins
An imprint of HarperCollinsPublishers

Original screenplay by
Harry Robertson and Harry Duffin.

This screenplay novelisation first published
in Great Britain by Collins 1997
3 5 7 9 10 8 6 4 2

Collins is an imprint of HarperCollins*Publishers* Ltd,
77-85 Fulham Palace Road, Hammersmith, London W6 8JB.

Copyright © Enid Blyton Ltd 1997

ISBN 0 00 675306-X

The author asserts the moral right to be
identified as the author of this work.

Printed and bound in Great Britain by
Caledonian International Book Manufacturing Ltd,
Glasgow, G64

CHAPTER ONE

"It looks just like England," Lucy-Ann said disappointedly to Philip, Dinah and Jack, looking round the baggage hall of Wellington airport. She hadn't quite known what to expect when they touched down in the capital of New Zealand after their long flight, but it certainly hadn't been this.

"All airports look the same nowadays," Bill Cunningham said, as he spotted their suitcases coming off the carousel. Bill was a tall, good-looking man who was shortly due to marry Philip and Dinah's mother, Alison. "C'mon, kids, don't just stand there. Help me get our luggage onto a trolley."

Lucy-Ann Trent took her holdall off the carousel and dumped it onto a trolley. She and her brother Jack usually stayed with Alison Mannering and her children in the holidays as they had no real home of their own.

"I want to see a koala bear!" Lucy-Ann said, with a look of delighted anticipation on her pretty face.

"You mean a kiwi!" said Philip. Philip was the tallest and strongest of the children, with short brown hair and brown eyes, and he had a real passion for animals. "The kiwi's the national bird of New Zealand."

"Kiki! Kiki!" chirped Kiki, Jack's pet parrot, which was sitting on his shoulder.

"Kiwi, Kiki, not Kiki!" Dinah laughed, and went over to help her brother, Philip, with his bag. Philip and Dinah looked very similar to each other although Dinah was shorter. However, they both shared the same determined look in their eyes.

A handsome man a few years younger than Bill strode forward to greet them. He was dressed in a smart suit and wearing an official pass allowing him access to all areas in the airport. The colour of his skin showed his Maori ancestry.

"You must be Mrs Mannering," he said to Alison, and shook the attractive blonde woman's hand and introduced himself as Dennis Turangi, an old friend of Bill's from way back. "Are you and Bill here on business?"

"Please call me Alison," Alison said and introduced him to Philip, Jack, Dinah and Lucy-Ann. "And yes, I am here on business. I've been asked to organise an exhibition of Maori art and craft back home in England."

"I'm part-Maori myself," Dennis revealed as he led them all through customs and to a waiting car. "My ancestor was a war chief."

"Really?" Philip asked keenly. This sounded interesting.

"The Maori were great warriors," Dennis told them, and by his side Bill grinned.

"Nothing's changed then!" he chuckled.

"Look who's talking!" Dennis said as he helped Alison to put her luggage in the boot of the car.

"Have you and Uncle Bill worked together before then?" asked Philip.

"Not exactly," Dennis replied. "It was Bill here who trained me."

"The hardest job I ever had!" Bill joked, and got into the car with the others.

*

"He is late!" The suave South American smashed his fist angrily onto the table. "I do not pay him tens of thousands of dollars for him to be late!" he snapped.

At the other end of the room, the man's assistant, Bruce, looked up from his seat in front of a wall of electronic equipment. He was a tough-looking Australian with a cruel face, both unshaven and unwashed.

"Fair suck of the sav, Mister Perez," he drawled. "Our contact's come a long way."

"I do not pay him to be late!" Perez repeated and paced up and down impatiently, glaring at the controls in front of Bruce, as if by watching them he could make his man appear. But although the equipment was a state-of-the-art tracking system, the screens – radio, radar and sonar – were all blank.

Perez turned on his heel and strode to the far end of the room where a metal gantry hung over an enormous tank of water. Swimming back and forth in the water was a huge shark. Perez suddenly smiled wolfishly: Pinky, his shark, his pet, was the one creature he could rely on – he was always hungry!

"Mister Perez, they're here!" Bruce said excitedly and pointed a stubby finger at the radar screen. A tiny blip had just appeared at the outermost edge of the screen, indicating the arrival of a small light aircraft.

A voice crackled over the radio. "*Viper* to *Espadon*, come in, please."

Perez grabbed the microphone. "*Espadon* to *Viper*, receiving you," he said. "Prepare to drop, I repeat, prepare to drop." He turned back to Bruce. "Are our men in the area?"

Bruce nodded. Divers in wet suits waited on four small motorboats near the drop site, ready to retrieve the plane's precious cargo from the ocean once the plane had dropped it.

"Excellent!" gloated Perez. Very soon the goods would be in his hands, and before much time had elapsed he would be millions of dollars richer.

Frano Wallace bobbed about in the ocean in his tiny cruiser and looked up at the cloudless sky. Frano was a tough-looking Maori in his late thirties and one of the best agents in the New Zealand security service. He'd been out here on the water for a couple of days, acting on a tip-off from one of his contacts in Colombia.

There'd been rumours for months now of a massive traffic in stolen art treasures between South America and New Zealand. The treasures, so the rumours went, would be stolen from museums and private art collections in both of the Americas. Then they would be brought here to New Zealand to be traded again for an enormous price to unscrupulous dealers and collectors the world over.

Frano even had the name of the person he suspected was the mastermind behind the thefts and their subsequent resales. But so far he hadn't one shred of proof, nor any idea of how the treasures were being brought into the country.

He heard the buzzing of a light aircraft, and shaded his eyes from the glare of the sun. The plane was flying much lower than it should be, and Frano realised in an instant what was about to happen.

The underbelly of the plane opened and a large object was jettisoned from the hold, landing with a mighty splash in the water only a quarter of a mile or so from Frano's cruiser.

Of course! This was how the art treasures were being smuggled onto the mainland! Dropped by plane into the sea and then picked up by divers!

This was his big chance! If he could only get to that crate before the divers then he'd have enough evidence to convict that scumbag, Emanuel Perez, for good!

Frano started to steer his cruiser

towards the site of the air drop.

Back at Perez's headquarters, Bruce was attending the tracking consoles, with Perez watching over his shoulder. Bruce grinned.

"Come on, boss," Bruce said. "You've gotta admit that five minutes late after seven hours' flying isn't so bad."

Perez grunted noncommittally. He was a fastidious man, and didn't like even the slightest thing to go wrong with his well thought-out plans. That was why he had evaded the law enforcement agencies of several countries for years now. He pointed at the radar screen.

"What's that?" he demanded.

Bruce peered at the screen. He saw the blip representing the aeroplane, as well as four other blips – one for each of the pick-up boats. There was also a sixth blip.

"An intruder!" he said, and switched open the two-way communications system. "Stinger One! Stinger One! There's a virus, ten degrees starboard! Capture!"

Perez snatched the mike from Bruce. "No, do not capture," he barked. "Terminate. I repeat, terminate!"

Perez and Bruce shared a sadistic smile. Whoever was out there didn't stand a chance.

CHAPTER TWO

Soon Alison, Bill, Dennis and the children were out of the airport and driving along the freeway towards their hotel in Wellington. All through the journey Dennis told the children the history of the Maoris, the original inhabitants of New Zealand. They now only formed about ten percent of the country's population, but they still possessed a vibrant and exciting cultural life. The hotel often staged demonstrations of Maori dancing and he advised them to check one out if they had the opportunity.

The hotel itself was a splendid affair, set in its own wooded grounds. The Arts Council, which was sending Alison on this trip, had certainly done them all proud. Jack's cheeky face lit up and he

16

made a mental note to explore those grounds later; they were sure to be full of all manner of exotic birds, and birds of all sorts were his obsession.

"Can I go swimming?" Dinah asked, noticing the large open-air pool in the centre courtyard.

"Later," Alison said, "when we've all caught up on our sleep." She led them to the doors of the lift which would take them up to their rooms, while a pair of hotel porters carried their luggage.

"But it's only the afternoon!" Lucy-Ann grumbled.

"And we've all been travelling for twenty-four hours," Alison pointed out.

"You'll have jet lag," Philip told her.

"I don't feel tired," Lucy-Ann said and pulled a sulky face.

"Don't worry – you will," grinned Alison.

"Good morning!" squawked Kiki on Jack's shoulder. "Good morning!"

Philip laughed. "Kiki's certainly not suffering from jet lag," he joked.

"That's because she slept all the way

over here," answered Jack.

"Jack, make sure you keep that bird quiet," Dinah said and then yawned, giving up on her idea of having a swim. "I'm going to try and get some sleep."

"Well, I'm not tired in the slightest," Lucy-Ann complained as the lift doors opened and Alison bustled them all inside. "I want to explore."

"You all have to stay in your rooms until dinner time," Alison said sternly.

"But that's wasting half a day," Lucy-Ann grumbled. She turned to the two boys. "Can I come over to your room and play a game?"

"No, you cannot," Philip retorted. "I'm not having you making a racket while I'm trying to sleep!"

"It's not fair," Lucy-Ann said. As the lift doors started to close, she glanced over at the bar area where Bill and Dennis were sharing a drink. "Bill's allowed to stay up!"

In fact, there was nothing Bill would have liked better than to have got some sleep, but there were more pressing matters to be attended to first. Although he was officially on holiday, his job in the Foreign Office meant that he was always on the alert for unusual situations, and he knew that Dennis was worried about one in particular. He sipped his strong black coffee while Dennis filled him in with what had been happening recently in his branch of the security service.

"We've got a bit of a problem – in fact, it's a very big problem indeed," he told his friend. "There's been a flood of stolen art treasures passing through here recently, but we can't seem to find the route."

"Do you have any idea who's behind this?" asked Bill.

"Our best bet is Emanuel Perez."

"Perez!" said Bill. "He's a nasty piece of work!"

To the general public Perez was simply a highly successful South American businessman and art lover. To the security forces, he was known as a ruthless criminal mastermind who had made a fortune several times over by stealing and selling priceless works of art. Despite this, Perez had never been caught. No one would dare to inform on him – not if they valued their lives.

"We know your boys back in England have been monitoring him for years," Dennis continued. "So we wondered if you could give us any pointers. His way of operating, that sort of thing."

"Dennis, if you want to stay healthy, stay well clear of Perez," Bill advised him.

"I can't, this time," Dennis said grimly. "Frano Wallace, one of our best agents, disappeared two days ago."

"While he was trailing Perez?" Bill asked and Dennis nodded.

Bill stroked his chin thoughtfully. "OK, Dennis, I'll tell you what I'll do. I'll have a word with my boss, Sir George Houghton, and I'll see if I'm security-cleared to give you all the information we have on Perez. It's not a lot – Perez is too careful for that – but it might help."

"I'd really appreciate it, Bill. It's time to nail Emanuel Perez once and for all."

"But remember, Dennis, that I'm here on holiday and am strictly non-operational," Bill continued. "I can't do anything which might put Alison and the kids in any sort of danger."

"I understand that, Bill."

"If it really is Emanuel Perez who's behind this art-smuggling operation," Bill said slowly, "he won't hesitate to kill anyone who gets in his way."

CHAPTER THREE

At the very moment that Bill and Dennis were talking about him, Emanuel Perez was sitting in his well-appointed office overlooking the sea. He picked up the photo of Bill and Dennis shaking hands which Bruce had secretly snapped at Wellington airport.

"Bill Cunningham," he said grimly. "So that's why that Maori agent was there to meet him."

"You know this Cunningham bloke?" Bruce asked, not really surprised. Mr Perez knew everything and everyone. It was how he stayed alive in this very dangerous game.

"I know of him," Perez replied. "He's a member of the British Special Services. So they've decided to bring him in, have they?"

"Maybe he's on holiday?" Bruce

suggested. "He had a sheila and a bunch of rug-rats with him."

Perez put down the photo and shook his head. He picked up a grape from a bowl on his desk and chomped thoughtfully on it.

"No, he's not on holiday," he stated confidently. "He's after me – he has been for years."

"So what do we do?" asked Bruce.

"First we must find out what he knows," Perez said. "And then you will persuade Mister Cunningham to 'disappear'."

An evil gleam appeared in Bruce's eyes. "Just say the word, Mister Perez," he smiled humourlessly. "It's always a pleasure to waste a pom!"

*

"I want to explore the hotel grounds," Philip announced the next morning when they'd all come down to the dining room for breakfast. "There must be zillions of unusual insects here."

Dinah pulled a face as she selected her breakfast from the wide variety on offer at the buffet. She hated talk of insects and creeping and crawling things at the best of times. She particularly didn't want to hear about them over her bacon and eggs.

"Well, if there are any, just don't bring them back here!" she said with feeling.

"Actually, I was thinking of putting them in your bed," Philip said, seemingly in all seriousness.

"Don't you dare!" Dinah squealed.

Alison laughed. "He's only winding you up," she told her as she made her way back to their table, where Bill was already tucking into his own breakfast. "Why do you always fall for it?"

"Because I don't trust him," Dinah replied simply, glowering at her brother.

Jack joined them at the table, with Kiki perched on his shoulder as usual. As he sat down, a fellow guest on the next-but-one table looked intently at him.

The stranger was probably in his early- to middle-forties, with a thin face, beaky nose, and long thinning dirty blond hair. He was an odd-looking, mousy sort of man, and there was something shifty in his eyes – or perhaps it was just that he was a little short-sighted.

Jack noticed nothing, and began to tell the others of his plans for the day.

"I'd like to see if I can find any of Kiki's relatives around here," he told them, and the parrot nodded her head as though she were agreeing with Jack.

"Whatever do you mean?" Alison asked.

"There used to be heaps and heaps of parrots here," Jack explained. "There aren't so many now, though, because they've almost been hunted to extinction."

Bill reached over and scratched Kiki behind her neck. "You'd better watch out, Kiki!" he joked. "We'll be changing your name to 'Dodo' soon!"

"Poor Kiki!" the parrot screeched in alarm. "Poor Kiki!"

Everyone laughed and returned to their meal. After they had finished, the girls went off to the hotel swimming pool, while Philip joined Jack and Kiki in the hotel grounds.

Sure enough there were many wonderful and unusual birds there, and the two boys were astonished by the wide variety and their splendid colours. There were even some fine-looking parrots, resplendent in their multi-coloured coats.

If Philip, Jack and Kiki hadn't been so interested in the birds, they might have spotted the blond-haired man from the hotel dining room now with them in the garden. Oddly, he was wearing a green anorak (even though the temperature was well into the seventies), and behaving rather strangely. He seemed to be following the two boys about.

Alison and Bill were sitting in the hotel lounge, talking to Dennis. He had brought Alison an old carved figure which had belonged to his father, and to *his* father before that. It was of an armed and snarling Maori warrior and, as Alison held it in her hands, she felt a shiver run down her spine.

"It's a beautiful piece," she admitted, "but it is a little scary." She passed it over to Bill to examine.

"That's what it's for, to be scary and fierce," Dennis told them. "It's meant to challenge both the living and the dead. Is it the sort of thing you're after, Alison?"

"Absolutely," she said enthusiastically. "If

you can spare it, it would be wonderful if you and your family could lend it to me."

"Sure," said Dennis. "No trouble."

Bill continued studying the figure. "Spirits are very important to your people, aren't they?" he said. "It's said that some of the old folks of your tribe had amazing powers."

"They had second sight and could read minds," Dennis agreed. "It is also said that some were also able to kill at a distance purely by using the power of thought!"

Alison shivered. "I just went cold all over!" she said, and then felt rather foolish and laughed.

Bill and Dennis joined in, and did not notice the figure of a burly Maori who walked past them. He was in the uniform of the hotel, though he was certainly not an employee. His reason for being in the hotel was simple: he was there to plant a bug in Bill's room so that Perez could keep track of Bill's movements.

Satisfied that Bill was deep in conversation with Dennis, and would be remaining in the lounge for some time, the man – whose name was Davey – took the lift up to the fifth floor where Bill's room was.

Using a pass key which he'd bribed a night porter into giving him, Davey entered the room. He wasted no time. He pulled out a chair and stood on it so that he could reach the lamp hanging from the ceiling. He took a small listening bug out of his pocket, and attached it to the lamp. Then he replaced the chair and left the room, leaving no evidence of his ever having been there.

CHAPTER FOUR

That evening the hotel was holding a demonstration of Maori culture in the dining room. Alison and the four children all settled down to see for themselves what Dennis had been talking about when he drove them back from the airport.

Some twenty Maoris, men and women, had turned up in their traditional costume and they were indeed a stunning sight to behold. Both the men and the women wore brightly coloured skirts which swayed this way and that as they performed their dance to the accompaniment of drums. They also wore long beads of greenstone and brightly-coloured coral, and the women wore large white flowers in their hair.

Most impressive of all were their painted faces. The men were decorated with a variety of painted patterns of lines and swirls and circles, giving them an imposing presence. Lucy-Ann even felt a little frightened, although she knew that the designs were traditional and had been handed down from generation to generation.

After the men had performed a "haka", which Alison informed them all was a traditional and highly impressive war chant, the Maori women took centre stage to sing an ancient song. Their voices were light and almost heavenly, and Lucy-Ann found herself thinking of the Maori women who had sung the very same song, way back before Europeans had ever discovered New Zealand.

"It's a pity Bill isn't here to see this," Dinah whispered as the women finished their song. The whole audience broke into spontaneous applause.

"Where is he, anyway?" asked Lucy-Ann, looking round.

"He's got another meeting with

Dennis," Alison told her.

"Dennis is a secret agent like Bill, isn't he?" Lucy-Ann asked, speaking loudly so that she could be heard above the noise of the clapping.

"Sshh, Lucy-Ann!" Alison said quickly, looking around to see who might have heard. Luckily no one seemed to be paying them any attention – except, perhaps, the strange man they'd all seen around the hotel and in the garden, the one with long blond hair and an anorak even though it was so warm. Odd how he always seemed to be nearby.

"I thought Bill was supposed to be on holiday," Philip said. Alison gave him a smile and sighed philosophically.

"He is," she said. "But you know Bill."

"Yeah, we sure do," Jack grinned, and then said, "Oh no! Look at Lucy-Ann!"

The Maori women had begun a dance, and in her seat Lucy-Ann was imitating their hand movements. Seeing this, one of the performers invited her to leave the audience and join them on the dance floor. Giggling, Lucy-Ann walked into the centre of the room, and started dancing with the other women.

"Typical!" Philip sniggered as he watched Lucy-Ann copy the women's graceful hand movements. Lucy-Ann had always enjoyed showing off. "You only have to open the fridge door and she'll do a tap dance!"

In his room, Bill looked up from a pile of faxes which Sir George had sent over to him after Bill had asked his permission to tell Dennis all they knew about Perez. Perez was a dangerous man, Sir George had agreed over the phone, and if Bill and Dennis could capture him then all the better.

"According to these faxes, Perez's usual style is to bring the stolen art out of South America across the Pacific," he told Dennis, who was sitting opposite him, poring over the pages of a large atlas.

Dennis drew a line with his finger from Colombia on the north-western coast of South America to New Zealand. "There are plenty of islands to string it through," he said. "The trouble for us is that we're so isolated here in New Zealand and the coastline's so difficult to patrol. He must be using a boat or a plane."

"Or both," added Bill. "You know, Dennis, I have a hunch that you could track this trail right into Perez's own backyard."

"You sound pretty convinced," Dennis remarked. He recognised that determined look in Bill's dark eyes.

"This art-smuggling racket smells like Perez," Bill said. "And I reckon that he ought to be nailed once and for all." He just wished he were in New Zealand alone – if he put one foot out of place with Emanuel Perez around, it could be disastrous for Alison and the children.

Perez, listening to Bill and Dennis on the newly-installed transmitter back in his headquarters, turned to Bruce, who had also been listening.

"I think it's time for Mister Cunningham to do his disappearing act, don't you, Bruce?" he asked.

Bruce nodded his head enthusiastically.

"Only it must look like an accident," Perez cautioned. "We don't want the whole of British Intelligence on our backs."

"Mister Perez – it will be my pleasure!" Bruce grinned. He loved killing people.

CHAPTER FIVE

An hour later, Bill waved goodbye to Dennis and decided to stroll through the hotel gardens before going in to bed. After an evening cooped up in a hotel room reading faxes, he could do with some air.

Philip and Jack were in their pyjamas at their bedroom window, idly watching the bird nightlife of the garden. They saw Bill in the gardens and thought nothing of it – until they saw something else.

"Who's that?" Philip asked urgently.

"Who's what?" Jack asked, and Philip drew his attention to a shadowy figure hiding in the bushes. They watched on in amazement as the figure began to sneak up on Bill. He was holding some sort of long stick in his hands.

35

"He's got a rifle!" Jack realised in horror.

"He's going to shoot Bill!" cried Philip. "Come on, we've got to save him!"

Philip and Jack raced out of their bedroom and through the reception area, nearly knocking over a cleaner doing the hoovering as they did so. They rushed out of the hotel doors and into the grounds. They looked round, but couldn't see Bill anywhere.

There was a movement in the bushes and they saw the shadow of the assassin. The man lifted up his rifle and prepared to take aim.

There wasn't a moment to lose. Philip and Jack ran towards the would-be killer and knocked him down in a classic double rugby tackle. The killer yowled with pain and surprise.

"Help! Murder!" he yelled out at the top of his voice.

He managed to shake Philip and Jack off and ran back towards the hotel, still clutching his rifle.

Just then Bill appeared, attracted by all

the noise and commotion. He took in the scene in an instant. "What's going on?" he demanded.

"He had a rifle!" Jack said, and pointed after the fleeing man. "He was trying to kill you!"

Not pausing to think why a thwarted murderer should try to find refuge in the hotel, the three of them gave chase. When they reached the hotel reception area, they found the long-haired, scruffy man from breakfast ranting to the unfortunate night porter. When he saw Bill, Philip and Jack he pointed accusingly at them with a long bony finger.

"Call the police!" he cried. "They tried to kill me! Get away from me, you villains! Get away from me!"

As Bill approached him he instinctively raised his rifle.

"Look out, Bill!" Jack called out.

Bill carried on walking calmly towards the man.

"It's all right, Jack," he said. "It's not a rifle."

"A rifle?" said the man in bewilderment.

"Of course it's not. It's a long-range microphone."

Philip and Jack saw that the man was right, and felt more than a little foolish. What had looked so menacing in the shadows they could see was now no more than a mike head attached to a long metal pole, which in turn was attached to a small tape recorder hooked on the man's belt.

Bill tried hard to resist a slight smile as he turned to the furious man with the microphone.

"What were you doing creeping about the hotel grounds at this time of the night?" he wanted to know.

"I was recording songs of the night birds, if you must know," the man replied indignantly. "And then these two young hooligans tried to kill me!"

"You're a bird watcher?" Jack asked in amazement.

The man peered down his long beaky nose to Jack. "Don't sneer, you young thug!"

"I wasn't," Jack said truthfully, who

loved bird-watching as well.

"My name is Horace Tipperlong," the man said proudly, trying to muster up some dignity. "And I'll have you know, you young hooligan, that I am very well known and highly respected in ornithological circles."

Bill could see that there was trouble coming. "I'm afraid there's been some misunderstanding," he said, attempting to defuse a potentially awkward situation.

"There's been a misunderstanding all right!" Tipperlong agreed angrily. "Letting young thugs like these two into respectable hotels: that's the misunderstanding! And I'm going to make sure that the manager hears all about it!"

With that, Tipperlong turned and marched off, holding his mike under his arm, just like a general leading his troops into battle.

"Oops," said Philip, when the bird-watcher had gone.

"It looked like a rifle," Jack said

earnestly to Bill. "Honestly."

Bill smiled. "Don't worry," he said. "It was an easy mistake to make." Then he added: "And I'm on holiday here, so there's no reason for anyone to want to get me. Is that clear?"

"That's clear," Philip and Jack said together. They would soon find out just how wrong Bill was.

CHAPTER SIX

The following morning, Philip and Jack weren't exactly the most popular guests at the hotel. True to his word, Tipperlong had informed the manager of the activities of the previous night and, as they entered the dining room for breakfast, the snooty manager had warned them that if there was a repeat of the previous evening's activities then they would no longer be welcome at his five-star establishment.

Tipperlong had also taken the greatest delight in telling as many as possible of his fellow guests about Philip and Jack. As far as he was concerned, they were juvenile delinquents, the scourge of all decent and respectable folk like him, the future downfall of the country.

The atmosphere at the hotel was tense, to say the least, and Bill suggested that they all went on a day trip to the nature reserve at Nga Manu. Philip and Jack could go looking out for all manner of animals, and Dinah and Lucy-Ann would enjoy a day away from the big city. Alison wanted to accompany them, but she had a meeting in town about the exhibition. She promised to meet up with them later for dinner.

So it was that Dennis picked them all up outside the hotel in a battered Jeep. Nga Manu was some way out of town along a wide cliffside road near the coast, so they settled down for a long drive.

On one side of them rose wooded hills. On the other side there was a steep drop to the beach and the sea far below. Lucy-Ann stared down at it from her seat, gulped, and decided that she'd turn her attention to the song Dennis was singing as he drove along.

What she missed seeing was another car, parked down on the beach. Bruce was climbing out of it and loading a rifle with a telescopic sight. When he saw the Jeep drive along the cliff road above him, he smiled and took careful aim . . .

"*Waiho ra!*" Dennis sang cheerfully. "*Ka tu tahi tahi-a-na.*"

"That's the Maori song they sang last night," Lucy-Ann realised, and Dennis wasn't surprised.

"It's a beautiful song," Dennis told them. "It's about the struggles and sacrifices that people have to make in order to achieve their dreams. Would you like to learn it?"

"Oh, yes, please! We'd love to," they all said together, and even Kiki squawked her agreement.

Dennis smiled. "OK, here's the first bit," he said, and sang the opening lines of the song again.

"*Waiho ra,*" everyone sang – except Bill.

"Come on, Bill!" said Dennis. "No party-poopers here!" So Bill joined in too. They were all really enjoying themselves.

Suddenly there was a loud noise

outside the Jeep and one of the front wheels exploded. The car immediately swerved violently off the road and plunged downhill with Dennis trying frantically to regain control, ever conscious of the extreme danger of their situation and the nearness of the cliff edge. Lucy-Ann screamed as she looked out of the window at the enormous drop to the beach below.

The other children sat frozen with fear. Kiki buried her beak in Jack's neck. Dinah banged her head as Dennis wrenched the wheel this way and that, and still the car continued on its deadly path.

Suddenly there was an enormous jolt as Dennis rammed his foot down hard on the brakes. The Jeep screeched to a halt just inches away from the edge of the cliff.

So abrupt was the stop that, despite his seat belt, Bill was flung forwards and cracked his head against the windscreen. He gasped with pain, and blood started to trickle down the side of his face.

Struggling to retain consciousness, he checked that everyone else was all right.

Dinah and Lucy-Ann were a little shaken, but were already clambering out of the rear doors along with Philip and Jack. Then, with Dennis's help, Bill climbed out too, trying not to look at the sickening drop below. He and Dennis looked around worriedly: they knew the sound of gunfire when they heard it, and the noise when the tyre burst sounded suspiciously like that.

Then they all heard the sound of an approaching car.

"Come on, Jack!" called Philip. "Let's go and stop that car!"

Philip and Jack rushed over to the road, and Bill wasn't fast enough to stop them. He just hoped it wasn't the gunman coming to finish off what he'd started.

The two boys saw a battered car come round the corner. They waved their arms frantically, trying to attract the driver's attention. Then they noticed, to their surprise, that their birdwatcher from the hotel, Mr Tipperlong, was at the wheel. Here at least was a familiar – if not quite friendly – face!

Tipperlong saw Philip and Jack trying to get him to stop, and snarled angrily. Rather than come to a halt, he pressed his foot down on the accelerator pedal and drove straight towards them. He wasn't going to pull up for two hooligans like Philip and Jack!

The boys leapt aside as the car flashed by them. Shocked and angry, they stared after the departing vehicle.

"That was Tipperlong!" Jack said. "Why didn't he stop?"

"More to the point, what's he doing here?" Philip wanted to know.

"There's a bird sanctuary somewhere near here," remembered Jack. "Maybe he's going there?"

"I wonder," said Philip and looked back to Bill and the others.

Dinah was attending to the cut on Bill's forehead, while Dennis was kneeling down and examining the burst front tyre.

"I'm going to have the tyres checked over, Bill," he said. "A burst tyre might have been an accident, but on the other hand . . ."

He didn't need to say any more. Philip and Jack exchanged sombre looks. They both knew that they had just survived an attempt on their lives. Someone was out to kill them.

But why? They desperately wanted to know. And was it just coincidence that Tipperlong was near the scene of the crime, or was his presence there something much more sinister?

CHAPTER SEVEN

"I'm fine, I tell you," Bill reassured Alison in his room after he had returned to the hotel. Above his head, the bug in the overhead lamp heard his every word and relayed them all back to Perez.

Alison looked unsure as she applied a sticking plaster to the small wound on his forehead. "Are you *sure* you're all right?" she asked again.

"It's just a graze, that's all," he told her, trying all the time not to show her how worried he was. Dennis had already sent the tyres off to be examined, and Bill was pretty sure that he already knew what would be the outcome of the forensic tests.

"You should take a rest," Alison told him.

"I intend to," he said. "Since you're working on the art exhibition I thought I'd hire a boat and take off for a couple of days."

"Where to?" asked Jack.

"Just lazing down south," Bill told him. "I'll probably do a bit of fishing. Maybe visit a couple of the small islands around here. Dennis has already a boat for me – it's called the *Lucky Star*."

"Can we come too?" asked Lucy-Ann as they all left Bill's bedroom and headed on down to the hotel lounge for some tea.

"Of course," Bill said, who knew that he'd be glad of the company. "I've already spoken to Dennis about it. As well as arranging the boat I'll be able to borrow some camping gear from him for all of us, so we can stay on the islands. And if you'd like to see some penguins we can go to Penguin Island . . ."

Lucy-Ann clapped her hands together in excitement. "Yes, please!" she said, and even Kiki seemed interested by the idea.

"You must be crazy to decide to go for a rest with this lot," Alison joked, and smiled at the children.

"We won't let him lift a finger," Dinah promised jokingly. "We'll wait on him hand and foot."

"I'll hold you to that, young lady!" Bill said, and then looked at Alison. "I wish you could come along as well."

"So do I," Alison replied. "But there's so much to organise for the exhibition."

Bill stood up. "Well, we'll leave you to it and get out of your hair," he said, when suddenly his mobile phone rang.

"Looks like you spoke too soon," Alison said, and the children's faces fell. Whenever Bill's mobile rang, they could be sure that it would be bringing news to hamper whatever plans they had.

"Dennis! How are you?" Bill said into the receiver, and then frowned when he heard what Dennis had to say to him. "OK, I'll be right there."

Bill switched off the phone, and then turned to the children with a serious look on his face.

"I suppose the boat trip is off then?" asked Dinah, fearing the worst.

"Not at all," Bill replied. "But you'll have to go down to the boat without me. I've got to see Dennis first of all. Alison, could you take the kids to the boat? I'll meet them there."

"When will that be?" Alison asked.

Bill shrugged his shoulders. "I don't know," he admitted truthfully, and handed Alison his mobile so that he could give her a ring to let her know. "I'll be there soon."

"You'd better be," Alison remarked. "I've got an appointment at the museum."

"No problem," Bill said. "Now, don't forget, the boat's called *Lucky Star*."

Once Bill had gone off to meet Dennis, Alison took the children down to the harbour, which was just a short cab ride from their hotel. At the jetty *Lucky Star* was there, and the boys rushed on board straight away to explore. Alison waited a while for Bill, but couldn't stay for long.

"Bye, Dinah. Bye, Lucy-Ann. I'm sorry I can't stay any longer." She looked pointedly at the boys. "Now, you two, don't wreck everything before Bill arrives."

"When's he coming?" Dinah asked.

"Any time now," Alison said, not having the faintest idea. Bill was notoriously hard to pin down, and Alison knew there was something strange going on. Why else would Bill be having all these meetings with Dennis?

"I wish you could come too, Aunt Allie," said Lucy-Ann.

"So do I, but I can't, Lucy-Ann," replied Alison. "I've got to get back. I'm supposed to be at the museum in ten minutes. Now, make sure you are all in bed by ten o'clock. Promise! And please behave for Bill."

Philip grinned. "If he's going to be our dad, he's got to get used to us, Mum."

"Philip!" Alison remonstrated. "Now, promise!"

"I'll keep them in order," Dinah said.

"You're sure you'll be OK?" said Alison, not wanting to leave them alone.

"We'll be fine," Dinah reassured her. "And we can always ring you on Bill's

52

mobile." She held out her hand, and Alison put the mobile into it. They all waved, and watched Alison till she was out of sight.

"Hey!" Jack said. "Do you see what I see?"

CHAPTER EIGHT

Dinah, Philip and Lucy-Ann looked around but saw nothing out of the ordinary.

"What do you mean, Jack?" asked Philip.

Silently, Jack pointed. Horace Tipperlong was carrying a box of baked beans along the jetty. He scowled at them as he passed by.

"Do you think he's following us?" Philip asked.

"Come on!" groaned Dinah. "Who'd want to follow *you*?"

Jack watched as Tipperlong searched amongst the boats moored up at the jetty. Finally he found the one he was looking for, and climbed aboard the small and slightly tatty boat that he had hired out.

"He *has* been acting pretty suspiciously," Jack pointed out.

"Boys!" Dinah said scornfully. "Why do they always have to make a mystery out of everything?"

"I know," Lucy-Ann agreed. "Perhaps Mr Tipperlong has hired that boat to take some time off like us. He's probably going bird-watching on one of the islands."

"Bird-watching! I can't think of anything more boring," Dinah said and then looked over at Kiki on Jack's shoulder. "Sorry, Kiki, no offence."

Kiki squawked huffily, while Philip and Jack shared a look which seemed to say: *Girls! They don't know anything!*

They were sitting on the deck of the *Lucky Star*, playing Scrabble and watching the other boats, when Philip saw Tipperlong's boat chug slowly out of the harbour and off to the open sea.

"I wonder where he's going?" he asked the others, and Dinah sighed and raised her eyes heavenwards. She'd had enough of Philip seeing mysteries where there weren't any.

"Philip, playing James Bond will not get you out of the washing up, you know!" she said.

Lucy-Ann had more important matters on her mind. She glanced at her watch and then looked wistfully towards the road leading down to the harbour.

"I wish Bill would hurry up," she said. "It'll be getting too dark to set off soon."

Bill looked grimly down at the photograph in Dennis's office. It was of a dead man, lying on a beach, his face half-buried in the sand.

"Where was he found?" he asked Dennis.

"Washed up on the beach a little way down the coast," Dennis told him. "We discovered him yesterday."

"And he's Frano Wallace, that agent of yours who went missing?"

Dennis nodded. "That's right," he confirmed. "Now, you know Perez. What I want to know from you is whether you think Perez is behind it."

Bill considered the photo for a few seconds more. "This isn't the way Perez normally works," he told Dennis. "Usually he's much more careful than this."

Dennis thought for a minute. "Perhaps they wanted us to know," he suggested.

"That's a possibility," Bill admitted. "It could be a warning – 'We killed Frano. You keep off or we'll do the same thing to you.'"

Dennis stood up and looked at the clock on the wall opposite. "You've done enough for us already, Bill," he said. "And the kids will be waiting for you on the *Lucky Star*. Let us deal with this now. Like you told me, you're non-operational here in New Zealand."

Bill was slightly reluctant to leave, but Dennis ushered him to the door.

"I just don't like leaving a case like this when a man has been killed," he told his friend.

"There's nothing else you can do," Dennis said reasonably. "You've given us some good leads."

"Not enough to pin Perez down, however."

"We're still very grateful, Bill, but we don't want you sticking your neck out especially with those young kids around. You just take a break for a few days, OK?"

Bill smiled. He knew that Dennis was right. A few days at sea would do him the world of good. His face beamed as he thought of the peace and quiet he, the children and Kiki would soon be sharing.

He couldn't have been more wrong. As he made the boat ready for sailing, with the children already in bed, Emanuel Perez and his henchman Bruce appeared at the jetty. Perez checked the small tracking screen which registered the information from the bug he'd had planted on *Lucky Star*. It pinpointed the boat's exact position.

"He's off," said Bruce.

"Perfect," replied Perez. "All on his own at sea. A perfect place for an accident with no witnesses."

CHAPTER NINE

The *Lucky Star* sailed peacefully in the ocean, alone and serene on an empty sea.

Philip was in the wheel house steering and Bill was watching over him, impressed by his ability to keep the boat sailing on an even and steady course. From the galley down below he could smell breakfast, and he licked his lips as Dinah came up carrying an enormous plate of bacon, eggs and toast.

"How wonderful!" he said, and thanked her. He left Philip alone with the steering and cheerfully tucked into the plateful.

"Where's mine?" a disgruntled Philip asked. "I'm starving."

"You'll have to wait," Dinah said. "You haven't been up all night, steering and keeping watch."

Bill yawned. It had indeed been a long night. Even though he'd returned quite late to the *Lucky Star* after his meeting with Dennis, he'd been as good as his word and got the boat out on the open sea that evening.

He knew that if they wanted to reach Penguin Island in good time to be able to set up their tents, then they'd have to keep to a very tight schedule. Consequently he'd spent much of the night awake at the wheel. Now he felt his sleepless night catching up with him.

He finished his breakfast, and yawned. "I'm going to have a nap," he told them all. "Will you be all right, Philip?"

"No problem, Skipper," said Philip, who was enjoying himself immensely at the wheel.

Satisfied that the boat was in capable hands, Bill retired below deck. As he did so, Jack finally staggered up the steps, wiping the sleep out of his eyes. He'd just woken up and Kiki was sitting on his shoulder, flapping her wings and generally giving him a good telling-off!

"Lazy bones!" she cackled. "Lazy bones!"

"Oh, do shut up, Kiki!" Jack said.

Lucy-Ann laughed, and then returned to looking out over the side of the boat and at the waves. "There's not another boat in sight," she said dreamily. "I bet we're the only ones for miles and miles around."

After a few more minutes, however, Lucy-Ann got tired of looking at nothing but sea, beautiful although it certainly was. She joined Philip at the wheel.

"Can I have a go at driving, Philip?" she asked.

"It's called 'steering', Lucy-Ann, not 'driving'," Philip said and sighed. Really, girls knew nothing at all! Nevertheless, he stood back and let Lucy-Ann take the wheel.

"What do I do now?" Lucy-Ann asked, and Philip sighed again. He pointed to a small panel on the dashboard in front of them.

"You keep that needle pointed in that

direction all the time," he instructed her.

"Is that all there is to it?" she asked, slightly disappointed that steering the *Lucky Star* was so simple. "What if there's a rock or something? Or a whale?"

"There aren't any rocks out here," Philip smiled. "And don't worry, the whales will get out of your way."

"Why's that?"

"They know you're steering, that's why!" he joked.

Before Lucy-Ann could give him a well-deserved punch in the ribs, Jack called them all over. He was sitting on the deck, scanning the horizon with the pair of binoculars he normally kept for bird-watching.

"There's a plane!" he told them. "It's flying really low."

Philip and Lucy-Ann shaded their eyes from the sun and peered into the distance. They could just make out the plane, and guessed it was probably about a mile or so away from their own position.

"Is it in trouble?" Philip asked Jack.

Jack continued to watch. The plane buzzed over the waves and then seemed to drop something into the water. Having done that, it gained altitude once more and sped off into the distance until Jack could no longer see it.

"It looked like it's just chucked something into the sea," Jack said, and lowered the binoculars.

"Why ever would it do something like that?" Lucy-Ann asked, just as puzzled as the two boys.

"I don't know," Jack admitted.

"Perhaps it was a trick of the light," Philip suggested.

Dinah came up from the galley. "Shall we sail over and see?" she asked.

"No, it's miles off," said Philip, who was much more eager to get to Penguin Island. "And it's not on our course."

"Shall we tell Bill?" Jack asked.

"He's fast asleep already," Dinah told them. "We'd better not wake him up until we reach the island."

*

Perez, too, was asleep when Dinah was

saying these words, but he came through to the control room in his silk dressing gown when his henchman Bruce buzzed him.

"What is the problem, my friend?" he asked.

"It's Cunningham," Bruce replied. "We've been keeping an eye on the tracking screen to see where he's going, and he's almost on top of the drop point. If he gets any closer, he'll see the whole operation!"

Perez frowned. "Are you sure?" he asked.

"No doubt about it at all," Bruce replied. "We've been tracking him for hours."

"Perhaps he knows more than he's telling anyone," said Perez, thinking aloud. Cunningham was a very dangerous man, and not to be underestimated.

"Just another fool like the last one, trying to make a reputation," sneered Bruce.

"Not so," said Perez. "Cunningham

already has a reputation. And he's no fool."

Bruce sat down and thought for a minute. "We'll have to turn *Viper* back," he said.

"No," said Perez sharply. "Leave everything as it is." He wasn't going to miss this drop just for one secret service man.

"But if he sees the drop, he'll tell his people!" cried Bruce.

Perez smiled nastily. "No," he said. "Cunningham is very thorough. He'll investigate first. And when he does we'll be there, with a reception committee."

"Great!" said Bruce. "Just the sort of party I like."

CHAPTER TEN

Lucy-Ann resumed her place at the wheel. They sailed for another hour or so, until Jack spotted a smudge of colour on the horizon.

"Land ho!" he cried excitedly and went on deck to tell the others.

"It's Penguin Island!" Dinah said, and found that she was just as excited as the two boys. "Wake Bill up so that he can sail us in."

"Land ho!" repeated Kiki. "Land ho!"

Once Bill had moored the *Lucky Star* in a small natural bay, the children all disembarked to take a look round. Penguin Island was a small rocky island which formed part of a chain of small islands in this part of the world. Some of them were quite sizeable, but others were so small that they weren't even recorded on any map. And although there were more beautiful places than Penguin Island, it was quiet and peaceful, which is what they all wanted.

It was also, Bill had assured them, teeming with wildlife. In the sky seagulls wheeled and turned while cormorants dived into the shallows, searching for fish. Of penguins, however, there wasn't a sign.

"I can't see any penguins at all," Lucy-Ann said.

Bill scratched his head, puzzled. "There should be thousands around," he said.

"Maybe they're all on the other side of the island," Jack suggested, although he couldn't make it out at all.

"Does anybody live here?" Dinah asked Bill.

"No, it's uninhabited," he replied and then looked at Philip who had spotted something on the ground. He knelt down and picked it up.

"Well, someone's been here," Philip said, and showed Bill the empty cigarette packet he'd found.

"It was probably thrown from a passing boat and washed ashore," Bill said.

"Or from that plane we saw," Lucy-Ann added.

Bill frowned. "What plane?" he asked. This was news to him.

"I saw a light plane about an hour ago while you were still asleep," Jack said and pointed in the direction from which it had come. "It seemed to drop something into the sea."

"What?" Bill was very interested indeed, though he tried not to show the children that.

Jack shrugged. "I don't know," he said. "It was too far away. But it seemed a bit odd, dropping something in the middle of the ocean."

"It was probably just a trick of the light," Bill said.

Dinah clearly didn't think that planes and mysterious objects which might or might not have been a trick of the light were particularly important.

"Shall we get the tents out?" she asked Bill.

"Yes, sure. Let's find somewhere to camp," Bill said and suggested that they walk a little way from the shoreline, but not so far that they'd get lost. "I'll go back to the boat and see if I can catch us all some fish for our supper tonight."

"And then afterwards we can go and see the penguins," Lucy-Ann said.

"If there are any," Jack corrected her. "I wonder what's happened to them all."

"We can worry about that later," Philip said. "Now, c'mon, everyone, let's find somewhere to camp!"

As Philip, Jack, Dinah and Lucy-Ann gathered up their camping equipment and tents and started to move off towards the interior of the island, none of them was aware that they were all being watched . . .

Bill sat on the edge of the *Lucky Star*, enjoying the warmth of the sun on his face, and the sound of the gulls in the blue and cloudless sky. He cast out with his fishing rod into the waves, and waited for the fish to bite.

He was relaxed and happy, and he realised that he had needed a break like this for a long time now. In fact, so relaxed and happy was he that he didn't even hear the sound of three wet-suited divers who had come up by the side of the *Lucky Star*. Nor did he notice the slight listing of the boat as they climbed aboard.

Bill got a bite. Grinning to himself, he stood up and tried to reel in his catch. Whatever it was he had caught was putting up quite a struggle, and it took him all his strength to pull it in. They were going to have a big fish supper tonight, Bill thought happily.

Someone tapped him on the shoulder, and Bill spun round. Who on earth could be on his boat with him? Surely one of the children couldn't have sneaked on board without him knowing? His heart lurched down to his stockinged feet when he saw the gun Bruce was pointing at his head. What a fool he'd been to believe that he was in no danger!

Another diver suddenly appeared from the other side of the boat, and Bill realised he really was in deep trouble. When a third diver climbed up the ladder to the aft deck, Bill knew he could do nothing. Even he couldn't tackle three thugs at once.

Bruce grinned in an evil way at Bill and took a waterproof two-way radio from the belt around his waist.

"*Stinger One* to *Espadon*," he said.

"*Espadon* to *Stinger One*," Perez's voice crackled over the airwaves. "Go ahead."

"The virus is caught. Returning to base on the *Lucky Star*."

Bruce closed down the connection and glanced at Bill, who was now being tied up by the two other men.

"You hear that, pom?" he said. "We're all going to take a nice trip in your boat to see Mister Perez."

Bill tried to keep his face blank as Bruce raised the anchor and started to steer a way out of the bay and back onto the open seas, though inside he was seething, both with fury at himself and with worry about the children. Had Bruce and his friend seen them on the island? Would they realise the children belonged to him? And if not, what would happen to Philip, Jack, Dinah and Lucy-Ann now, stranded on a deserted island, alone and with no means of escape?

CHAPTER ELEVEN

Bruce and the two thugs steered the *Lucky Star* to a small island about three hours' sailing time from Penguin Island. Armed guards patrolled the island's small jetty, and as Bill was led to the fancy-looking house which dominated the north face of the island, he guessed that this was probably Perez's very own private island. The crook must have made millions from his art thefts over the years, he realised.

Bill was taken to the huge tank room, where Perez was waiting for him. From behind the plate glass walls of the tank, the shark looked out hungrily at Bill. There followed a very unpleasant period of questioning by Perez, and violence by Bruce, who was thoroughly enjoying himself. Bill was tied to a chair.

"What else did their agent tell you, Mister Cunningham?" Perez demanded for what seemed the umpteenth time. "Before we killed him, that is."

Bill didn't answer, and stared hatefully at Perez. There was a trickle of blood on Bill's face from where Bruce had hit him. The rough Australian raised his arm to strike him again, but Perez halted him.

"Who else knows about my presence here?" Perez asked. "Is there anyone else on the island?"

"No. I came here on my own," Bill lied, desperately hoping that Perez would believe him, and that he could conceal the children's presence from the South American. "There's no one and nothing on Penguin Island. There aren't even any penguins!"

Perez smirked. "Of course not," he said. "I had my men get rid of them. Very good target practice! Too many people were coming to the island to see the penguins. I couldn't have that! Penguin Island is too near my base of operations. Is that why you came to the island, Mister

Cunningham? To spy on me?"

"No," said Bill. "I needed a rest."

Bruce grinned. "You'll get a rest all right, pommy," he promised. "A real long one." He turned to Perez. "Shall I feed him to Pinky?" he asked eagerly.

Perez shook his head. "No. We'll let him sleep on it," he said. "Perhaps tomorrow your memory will be better, Mister Cunningham."

"You're going to kill me anyway, Perez," Bill said defiantly. "You'll get nothing out of me!"

"We shall see, Mister Cunningham, we shall see." Perez crossed over to the bank of controls and scanning equipment which lined the wall opposite the shark tank.

"Shall I order the drop for tonight, Mister Perez?" Bruce asked.

The South American looked up from the instruments and shook his head. "Cancel it," he told him. "There's a major storm brewing."

Jack scanned the horizon with his

binoculars, then shook his head and returned to the others who were sitting on the beach.

"There's no sign of either Bill or the *Lucky Star*," he told them sadly. He handed the binoculars over to Dinah who had a look as well, but the sea was quite empty.

"Where can he be?" she asked, and the worry was evident in her voice.

"He'll be back," Philip said with a certainty he definitely didn't feel.

"Perhaps he just wanted to have some time on his own," Dinah said. "He is supposed to be having a break."

"I guess we can be something of a handful at times," Philip admitted.

"Well, when he gets back everybody has to be especially good and not be a nuisance," Lucy-Ann decided.

"And that includes you, Kiki!" Jack said.

"Wipe your feet!" the parrot kaw-kawed. "Blow your nose!"

Philip pointed up to the approaching mass of dark clouds on the horizon. "I think we'd better get back to our camp," he told them all. "It looks like there's going to be a storm. The sooner we get under shelter the better."

The children had set up their two tents in a small wooded clearing a few minutes' walk from the beach. In the short time they took to reach their campsite, the rain had started to fall and a breeze was blowing up. They hurriedly climbed inside and fastened everything as securely as they could, but within minutes the rain had become a torrent and the breeze a gale. Lightning forked and cracked in the sky and thunder boomed so loudly that it sounded like giant cymbals.

The wind lashed mercilessly at the two tents and Philip only hoped that they'd pegged them down securely enough. It hadn't occurred to the children when they were putting them up that a storm this ferocious would get up so suddenly. If the tents were to blow away then they'd have no shelter from the storm. Philip had heard about tropical storms and knew just how vicious they could be. They wouldn't stand a chance out in the open.

It was all too much for Lucy-Ann, who hated storms at the best of times. She left her own tent, and joined the boys and Kiki in theirs. Dinah wasn't slow to follow her, and all four of them huddled together.

"I'm scared!" wailed Lucy-Ann.

"There's nothing to be scared of," Philip insisted fervently, raising his voice so that it could be heard above the howling of the wind and the flapping of the tent.

"Oh yes there is," Lucy insisted with an equal fervour. "Uncle Bill's missing, and we're stranded on a deserted island in these little tents in the middle of a huge storm!"

"Put like that, I guess she does have a point. . ." Jack said. He was holding down one of the four corners of the tent in an effort to stop it from being blown away.

"This is no time for jokes!" Philip snapped in an uncharacteristic outburst of bad temper.

"What about the other tent?" Dinah asked. "It might blow away."

"We'll have to leave it!" Philip said as he attempted to hold down his own corner of tent. "At least the four of us can hold down this one."

But he spoke too soon. Suddenly there was a massive rush of wind and their tent was torn free of its moorings. Jack and Philip were unable to hold on any longer and Lucy-Ann screamed as the tent was blown away and the tent poles came tumbling down around her. Now they had no shelter and nowhere to go. Whatever were they going to do?

CHAPTER TWELVE

Struggling to keep their balance in the roaring gale, they headed for the girls' tent, only to see that one being blown away by the wind as well. It was so strong that it was almost impossible to stand.

"Hold hands, everyone!" cried Philip. "We've got to find shelter!"

They staggered off, bent double against the mighty force of the wind. Kiki hid inside Jack's jacket, out of the rain which was starting to soak them all through to the skin. Nobody quite knew where they were heading – they'd explored most of the island already, but had seen no kind of shelter.

"It's hopeless, we'll never find anywhere!" Dinah said despairingly as they approached a small hillside. Philip pointed through the driving rain.

"Oh no?" he said, and grinned. "Then what about that?"

A small hut was nestling against the hill. It looked ramshackle and rickety but it was at least holding up much better to the storm than any of them were.

"I thought the island was deserted," Lucy-Ann said as they all ran towards it.

Dinah peered in through a dirty and cracked window. It was dark and empty inside, with a few pieces of strange-looking furniture scattered around.

"There's no one there," she said.

"Let's go in," decided Philip and walked over to the wooden door. It was unlocked and he opened it.

"We shouldn't," Jack said cautiously. "It must belong to someone."

"But Bill said nobody lived here," Dinah reminded them.

"We've got to get out of this storm!" Philip said decisively and entered the hut. "Come on!"

"It smells funny," Lucy-Ann said once

they were inside. She squinted in an effort to accustom her eyes to the darkness.

"Wipe your feet!" said Kiki. "Blow your nose!"

"I wonder where Bill is," Jack said, voicing all their thoughts.

"I hope he's not out on the sea in this storm," Philip said, and shuddered. Even an expert sailor would be in trouble in the middle of the very strong wind and rain.

Jack reached into his pocket and drew out a box of matches. He struck one and they looked round their new shelter. It was sparsely furnished, with just a few old chairs and a table. On the wall there hung Maori carvings and ceremonial masks.

Suddenly Lucy-Ann screamed. Everyone turned and looked in the direction in which she was pointing.

Staring at them through the window was a wild and frightening face. Big bulging eyes glared in a face lined with elaborate designs and decorations. The face bared its teeth at them in a grimace, then moved away from the window and walked over to the door. The handle turned and the door began to open.

The children and Kiki watched fearfully as the newcomer appeared. He was a big, powerful-looking Maori, wearing a long flax jacket and ornaments of greenstone and whalebone round his neck. He was leaning on an old gnarled stick.

It was his face-painting which had made him appear so frightening to Lucy-Ann, but even now, as she watched him light an oil lamp, he still carried about him an air of power and authority. He lit the lamp, and then regarded each of them in turn, without saying a word. He gave them all a look which sent shivers down their spines.

"Ha-hallo. Our tent blew away and—" Jack was very nervous.

Philip said: "Is this your place...?"

"We had to get out of the storm," Dinah explained. They all took a step backwards as the Maori entered the room.

"Please, if we're trespassing or something—" Jack began and then fell silent.

The Maori considered him thoughtfully for another few moments, and then smiled.

"I am Te Araki, and this is my whare," he said, gesturing about the room. "And you are all welcome here."

The four children and Kiki breathed a sigh of relief, especially when Te Araki went over to a tiny stove and put the kettle on. Four hot cups of sweet tea later and things were beginning to look a little better. Even the storm outside showed signs of abating and the Maori assured them that it would be over by morning. They could stay in his shack tonight, if they liked, and return to their campsite at first light tomorrow.

"Bill should be back by now," Lucy-Ann told Te Araki. "He went out in a boat."

Te Araki was silent for a moment and his big eyes seemed to stare into the distance. "Your friend is in trouble," he said finally.

CHAPTER THIRTEEN

"Bill's in trouble? What sort of trouble?" Philip asked urgently.

"He is with evil men, on an island not far away from here," Te Araki informed them.

"How can you know that?" Jack asked, with just the slightest trace of suspicion in his voice.

"Te Araki knows everything," was the mysterious reply. He placed his hand on his chest. "Both here," he said, referring to his heart, and then placed his hand on his head. "And here."

Dinah leant forward. She was fascinated by this strange man. "Who are you?" she asked. "What are you doing here?"

"For some time I felt that there was

something wrong on the island," Te Araki said. "And so I came to see."

"There *is* something wrong," Lucy-Ann said. "There are no penguins, for one thing."

"That is right, my child. I believe the evil men may have driven them away."

"Why?" Jack wanted to know.

"I wait to see," Te Araki said. "And to see if the penguins will return."

"How did you know that something was wrong?" Dinah asked.

"My people are very close to nature," Te Araki told her. "We know many things that men in the cities have forgotten."

"Like being able to see things in your mind?" asked Lucy, who by now was just as fascinated as Dinah.

"Aye, and to live with the world, little one. We have a song that tells that the storm outside will clear away the dead and the weak, leaving the strong to grow on."

"We know a Maori song," Lucy-Ann said proudly.

"*Kia ora! Weha tu mai!* Sing it for me!"

Te Araki demanded.

The children looked at each other, a little embarrassed. Te Araki just waited and eventually Lucy-Ann started to sing the song which Dennis had taught them on the way to the nature reserve. Philip, Jack and Dinah looked at each other again, then joined in too. Even Kiki provided a counterpoint to their harmonies.

Te Araki listened, a smile filling his face from ear to ear. When they had finished he clapped his hands, got to his feet and sang a haka, a traditional war chant. Kiki joined in, bobbing up and down and raising her crest. She looked so comical that they all laughed, forgetting their troubles for the moment.

Te Araki was suddenly serious. "And like the sea lion we will have to be quick, if we are to find your friend Bill," he said.

"You mean you'll help us find him?" Lucy-Ann asked delightedly.

"Yes," replied Te Araki. "But not now. You must all get some rest. We start at first light tomorrow!"

The storm had devastated the children's campsite, as they discovered when they and Te Araki visited it the following morning. Jack's camera and Dinah's Walkman were broken and covered in mud. One tent hung several feet up from a nearby tree, while the other one was nowhere to be found.

"Never mind about your Walkman!" Jack scolded Dinah after she'd spent an unsuccessful five minutes trying to repair it. "Try and find some food – I'm starving!"

Lucy-Ann had spotted a bag. "Look!" she cried. "Potatoes!"

"Great – chips for breakfast," Jack said to Philip, who was busy trying to light a fire. "Allie and Bill would have a fit!"

Philip finally managed to coax the fire into life and a small cloud of smoke appeared, along with a few flames.

"Smoked chips at that," giggled Dinah.

Te Araki, who had gone down to the beach to see if he could find anything to eat, reappeared. He was carrying a taiaha, which he had explained to the children was a carved Maori weapon, shaped like a long stick. He was also carrying a brown paper bag.

"*Ki-ora!*" he said, using the traditional Maori greeting.

"*Ki-ora!*" replied Philip. "What's in that bag?"

"*Cremon* – breakfast!" Te Araki told them and opened up the bag to reveal its contents.

The children all pulled a face when they saw the sea urchins inside, looking decidedly inedible. What they wouldn't have given for a nice juicy steak and chips right now!

After the breakfast (most of which the children didn't eat), Te Araki set them all about their individual tasks. Dinah and Lucy-Ann were to light a beacon to attract the attention of any passing boat or plane. It was vital for them to get news about Bill's disappearance over to the mainland as soon as possible.

Jack was entrusted with keeping a look-out on the beach, while Te Araki instructed Philip in the use of the taiaha.

The taiaha was now only used in Maori ceremonies, Te Araki told him, but in earlier days it had been a fearsome weapon. Philip could well believe it as he watched the Maori wave it around with all the skill and precision of a baton carrier in a big parade, or an expert player in a fast-moving kendo game, like the ones he'd often seen on the cable sports channel.

"All combat is about balance as much as brute force," Te Araki told him. "It is about being one with the weapon. *A na!*"

He raised the taiaha and brought it down on Philip's head, stopping when it was mere inches away from his skull. Philip was amazed by the man's control, and, for one so burly, he was surprisingly nimble on his feet. Te Araki handed the taiaha over to Philip and urged him to try out his own skill.

After a few practice twists and turns Philip took to the weapon like a natural.

"Ka pai! Ka pai!" Te Araki congratulated him. "You have a good arm."

Philip's chest swelled with pride and he tried a few further swipes, nearly decapitating Dinah, who was piling driftwood up on the beacon.

"Look out, you idiot!" she cried.

Te Araki smiled, and took the taiaha from Philip before he could do any more damage.

"Control, my child," he told him. "Control is the secret of battle."

At that moment they heard Jack call out to them from his vantage point on the beach, and they all ran down to join him. He was pointing out to sea at a familiar boat which was coming in to land.

"It's the *Lucky Star*!" Jack said.

CHAPTER FOURTEEN

Lucy-Ann whooped with delight and jumped up and down, waving at the approaching craft.

"Uncle Bill! Uncle Bill!" she called out, even though she knew that the boat was still too far out for anyone on board to hear her.

"Silly Billy!" screeched Kiki. "Silly Billy!"

A worried look appeared on Te Araki's face. "You must hide," he told them sternly.

"But it's Bill," Philip protested.

"No, it is not," he said and in answer to their question of how he could know he merely replied: "I know."

The children all looked at each other, unsure what to do.

"Go to the hut!" There was something in the man's voice which told the children that he wouldn't take no for an answer.

"Come on, Lucy-Ann," Philip said when she started to protest. "Let's do as he says." He turned and ran off in the direction of Te Araki's shack.

Lucy-Ann and Dinah followed him, but Jack stayed by the water's edge for a minute. He took out his binoculars and raised them to his eyes.

Sure enough the boat was the *Lucky Star* but, as Te Araki had said, Bill wasn't on board. Instead, Bruce and Davey, the man who'd placed the listening bug in Bill's hotel room, were steering the boat into harbour. They were both carrying rifles.

Jack turned and followed the others. As he did so, he looked around for Te Araki. The Maori seemed to have disappeared into thin air. Realising that he'd have to worry about his whereabouts later, Jack raced back to the hut.

"Two men with guns!" he panted, as he

caught up with the others back at the hut.

"We'd better hide!" Dinah said.

"Where's Te Araki?" asked Philip, noticing the older man's absence for the first time.

"He's vanished," Jack said. "And so has Kiki."

In fact, Kiki hadn't vanished at all. In all the excitement she'd flown off Jack's shoulder and perched on the topmost branches of a tree, just as the *Lucky Star* moved into the bay. She watched while Bruce and Davey disembarked, their rifles at the ready.

Davey was the first on shore. He surveyed the beach, looking for any sign of life.

"Somebody must be around here, somewhere," the Maori said to his Australian companion.

"It shouldn't be too hard to find them," Bruce said. "Mister Perez is sure that Cunningham isn't working alone. They're bound to be holed up somewhere here."

"Hide! Hide!"

"Who's that?" Bruce said, and looked

all around him. There was nothing to be seen except for the seagulls.

"Who's that?" repeated Kiki, hidden high in the tree. "Who's that?"

"It sounds like the birds are talking!" Davey said.

"It's a trick!" insisted Bruce angrily.

"Silly Billy! Silly Billy!"

"OK, pal, if you want to play games . . ." Bruce said and walked up the shore, his eyes darting this way and that.

Still he couldn't find anyone and he gestured to Davey to follow him further into the island. It was only a matter of minutes before they discovered the ruins of the children's campsite.

"See, I told you there was someone here!" Bruce said to Davey, and then spotted Te Araki's hut in the distance.

"That's where they must be," Davey said and started to stalk towards the old shack.

"And remember," Bruce said with an evil grin on his face. "If anyone is in there, we shoot to kill!"

Davey peered in through the dirty and

cracked window of Te Araki's shack. The place seemed to be empty.

The children were as still as statues inside their hiding places. Lucy-Ann was hiding in a large chest. Dinah was curled up under the rickety table, Philip was in the cupboard and Jack was hiding under a piece of flax, in the middle of the floor. The children all held their breath, knowing that one sudden noise or movement would alert the men to their presence.

"There's no one in here," they heard Davey say. "Let's go."

"Hah!" said Bruce. "We'd better check it out even so."

Inside the hut the children listened with horror as they heard the door handle being turned and the door creaking open.

Suddenly there was a most terrible blood-curdling roar. Bruce and Davey spun round on their heels to see Te Araki outside, looking fierce and waving his taiaha in their direction. His eyes were rolling madly and his tongue was stuck out at the two intruders as he went into a frenzied war dance, leaping, chanting and gesturing.

"Strewth!" Bruce said. "The cracked old goat startled me for a moment there!" He raised his rifle, making to shoot the chanting newcomer.

"No!" said Davey, the Maori in him rebelling. "It's bad luck."

Bruce sniggered and prepared to pull the trigger. "Yeah, bad luck for him," he said.

Davey knocked down Bruce's rifle. "No, he's a tohunga -- a holy man," the Maori explained. "It's bad luck if we harm him."

Bruce watched as Te Araki continued his war dance. "Well, I guess the mad old ponga's harmless enough," he said at last and shouldered his gun.

"This must be his place," Davey guessed. "That's why he's getting angry."

Bruce looked back at the hut. As far as he was concerned it was a dump. "Well, he's welcome to it," he said. "Come on, let's get back on the water."

After the men had gone, Te Araki

entered the shack and everyone started to congratulate him on his quick thinking. It was only his appearance that had stopped Bruce and Davey from searching the shack and discovering their hiding places.

"No time, no time," he said. "We must make up the fire again, when the bad men have gone. We must get help."

"But surely you have a radio?" Jack asked. Te Araki shook his head.

"I came to Penguin Island to live with nature," he told him. "I wanted to cut myself off from the outside world for a while."

"But you must have a boat," Dinah reasoned. "Otherwise how could you have got to Penguin Island in the first place?"

"A friend brought me here, and then sailed off back to the mainland," Te Araki said. "He will return in about a month's time."

Help, in fact, came much sooner than any of them could have anticipated, and in the most unexpected form imaginable.

After half-an-hour's work on the beacon, Philip and Jack had managed to get quite a good fire going and were using a blanket to create smoke signals. Everything seemed to be going well and even Kiki had returned from her temporary absence.

Philip and Jack were looking skywards in the hope of seeing a plane. Lucy-Ann watched the ocean and very soon caught sight of a small boat approaching the bay.

"We've done it!" she cheered. "We've done it."

"No, we haven't," Jack said grimly after he had raised his binoculars to his eyes and recognised the approaching boat. "It's that man Tipperlong."

"Tipperlong! What's he doing here?" asked Philip.

"Good question," said Jack, who had always harboured suspicions about the so-called ornithologist.

"Is he alone?" Dinah asked, and Jack nodded. He couldn't see anyone else in Tipperlong's ramshackle boat.

"Maybe he's in league with those other

two men?" Philip said.

"Then we'd better hide," Lucy-Ann said wisely.

"I've got a better idea," said Jack. "When he gets ashore, why don't we nab his boat?"

CHAPTER FIFTEEN

Jack and Kiki hid in the bushes near the harbour as Tipperlong anchored his boat out in the bay and lowered a small motorboat into the water to cross the short distance to the shore.

Jack had to admit that Tipperlong didn't particularly look like a dangerous enemy agent, but he knew all too well that appearances could be deceptive. They would have to wait until he was out of the way before they could commandeer his boat.

When Tipperlong reached the beach he immediately noticed the smoke from the beacon at the top of the hill, and wandered up to it. To do this he had to take a turning which effectively meant that he could no longer see his motorboat moored in the harbour below. It was the chance that Jack was waiting for.

As soon as Tipperlong was out of sight, Jack left his hiding place and signalled to the others, who had taken cover behind a group of rocks. They all raced on down to the boat at the water's edge.

Tipperlong's motorboat seemed barely seaworthy, but it was the only chance they had.

"You start it, Phil," called Jack. "I'll keep watch."

Philip wrestled with the engine. He pulled the cord twice, but nothing happened. He pumped fuel into the engine and tried again. Nothing happened.

"Come on, Phil!" cried Jack. "Get her started!"

"I'm trying," Philip answered, and finally the engine fired.

Tipperlong, standing up by the beacon on the hill, heard the sound of his motorboat and started to rush down to the beach.

"That's my boat!" he called out. "Leave

it alone!"

Just as he reached the shore the girls succeeded in pushing the boat away with two boat hooks. The engine failed and they drifted, but it caught again the next time Philip tried, and finally he was able to point it out to sea.

What he saw was not a sight he wanted to see: the *Lucky Star*, with Bruce and Davey aboard, attracted by the beacon smoke, had turned round and was heading back to the island!

"You hooligans!" Tipperlong called out ineffectually as he watched his boat pull away. "You can't steal my boat!"

"We're only borrowing it," Jack called back.

"What have you done with Uncle Bill?" Dinah cried out as the motorboat moved further away.

"Uncle Bill? Who's Uncle Bill?"

"Don't play the innocent with us!" Jack said.

"I don't know what you're talking about!" Tipperlong shouted and stamped his feet in fury on the beach. "You're all mad!"

Ignoring Tipperlong's protests, Philip looked away to the north of the island. The *Lucky Star* was rounding a corner now, and the little motorboat would soon be in full view.

"They'll spot us!" Dinah gasped.

Philip indicated a small rocky outcrop a little way off, and steered towards it. "We can hide over there," he told them. "And then wait for the *Lucky Star* to leave."

"But what about Te Araki and Mister Trip-a-lot?" asked Lucy-Ann.

"Those guys won't harm Te Araki, and as for Tipperlong we don't care," Jack said. "His friends will help him now."

"His friends?" Lucy-Ann wasn't quite sure what Jack was talking about.

"Those guys on the *Lucky Star*," Jack said. "It can't be a coincidence that Tipperlong's on the island at the same time. He has to be in cahoots with them."

Philip successfully piloted the motorboat behind the cover of the rocks just as the *Lucky Star* moored in the harbour. Bruce and Davey took out their rifles and came ashore once more. Tipperlong was still on the beach with his back towards them.

"Watch yourself," Bruce advised Davey as they drew closer to the bird-watcher. "These pom secret service agents are trained killers."

They silently approached Tipperlong, like big cats stalking their prey. Tipperlong still hadn't registered their presence behind him, which Bruce thought was a little unusual. These secret service guys were supposed to have razor-sharp reflexes and instincts.

"Freeze!" he growled, and aimed his rifle directly at Tipperlong, who turned round. The moment he saw the rifle he raised his hands high above his head.

"Oh no! Please don't shoot!" he pleaded. "Please don't shoot!"

Bruce's face fell and there was a puzzled look on his face. This sort of reaction hadn't exactly been the one he'd been expecting.

"I beg of you!" Tipperlong said and

then stamped his foot in frustration. "I really can't take any more of this." He lowered one arm so that he could pull a handkerchief from out of his pocket and wipe the tears from his eyes.

"What dung heap did they drag you from?" Bruce demanded, although he didn't lower his rifle. Bill Cunningham's men were devious so-and-sos, he'd heard, and Tipperlong's cowardly behaviour could be a bluff.

"S-sorry? I don't understand. . ."

"Come on, jelly, we're going to take you to your mate," Bruce said, and prodded Tipperlong with the barrel of his rifle.

"Mate?" repeated Tipperlong. He was now even more confused.

"Watch this one," Bruce whispered to Davey as they led him down to the water's edge. "He's a wily old devil, that's for sure!"

As Bruce and Davey roughly bundled Tipperlong aboard the *Lucky Star*, the children watched on in amazement from their hiding place behind the outcrop.

"He can't be with them!" Philip gasped. "They've both got their guns on him!"

"So who is he?" Jack asked.

Dinah looked at him in superior fashion. "Have you never thought that he might just be a harmless old bird-watcher after all, Jack?" she asked wearily and with more than a little bit of sarcasm.

"So what do we do now?" Lucy-Ann asked, turning the conversation to much more practical matters.

"We see where they go," Jack told them all. "Because wherever they go then that's where Uncle Bill is sure to be!"

CHAPTER SIXTEEN

Standing on the highest point on Penguin Island, the same place where they had lit the beacon, Jack tracked the progress of the *Lucky Star* through his binoculars. It was obvious that Bruce and Davey were heading for one of the many small islands on the horizon but it was essential that they discovered which one.

Finally, when the *Lucky Star* was so far away that Jack was scared he would lose sight of it even with his binoculars, he saw it slow down and approach one tiny island to the north-east. He put down his binoculars and pointed out the island to the others.

"That's where they're going to!" he said confidently.

"Then that's where Uncle Bill must be!" said Lucy-Ann.

"Now we can go and get help," said Dinah.

"Go to the mainland?" asked Philip and shook his head. "It would take too long. We've got to try and rescue Bill on our own."

"And find some food!" said Jack, whose stomach had been rumbling for some time now.

"Pieces of eight!" squawked Kiki, cheered by the mention of food. "Pieces of eight!"

Lucy-Ann and Philip chuckled at the sight of Kiki on Jack's shoulder. "You'll have to get an eyepatch, Jack," Philip joked.

"And a wooden leg!" added Lucy-Ann.

"How are we going to get to the island?" Dinah asked Philip and looked dubiously at Tipperlong's small motorboat. They'd already seen just how unreliable its engine was and Dinah doubted that it would carry them all the way to the island.

Philip pointed out to where Tipperlong's larger boat was moored out at sea. "We'll use the motorboat to get us there, and then take the larger boat for the rest of the journey," he told her.

"Are you sure you can drive Tipperlong's boat, Philip?" Dinah asked.

"Of course I can!" said Philip, slightly put out that his nautical skills were being called into question.

"And it's called 'steering', not 'driving'," Lucy-Ann pointed out to Dinah rather smugly.

Philip was as good as his word and soon they were sailing in the much larger boat towards Perez's island. While he steered and Lucy-Ann helped with the navigation, Dinah and Jack got down to the more urgent task of finding something to eat. In the cupboards of the cramped galley they found nothing but –

"Baked beans!" Dinah groaned as she pulled out yet another tin.

"Trust us to hijack a vegetarian's boat!" Jack said, but couldn't resist a smile in spite of his empty stomach.

"There's no time to eat anyway, you two!" Philip called out. "We're nearly there!"

Dinah and Jack came up on top to see the approach to Perez's island. Philip had correctly assumed that the harbour would be patrolled by guards, and so he had sailed round the back of the island to a small pebbled beach where they anchored, leaving Kiki to guard the boat.

"I wonder what they're up to?" Lucy-Ann wondered as they tramped over the beach.

"Something illegal, that's for sure," Philip said.

"Which way are we going?" asked Dinah.

"There's only one place they could be hiding Bill," Jack said and gestured to the large building at the top of the hill.

"How can you know that?" she asked.

"It's the only building on the island," he told her. "And besides, it's surrounded with a high wire fence. That seems a pretty convincing argument, doesn't it?"

"So how do we get up there?" Philip asked.

"We go right through the middle," Jack replied and pointed out what looked like a trail winding its way up to the top of the hill.

"It's a very steep climb," Lucy-Ann said doubtfully.

"It's a bit exposed as well," Philip remarked and looked around to check that there weren't any armed patrols of guards in the area. "We'll have to be very careful."

They started the long hike up the hill to Perez's headquarters. When they were about halfway up, they saw the reason for the absence of guards at the rear of the building.

Down below them they could see the jetty where the *Lucky Star* was moored. Another boat – Perez's own boat, the *Espadon* – was also moored there, and most of the guards seemed to be occupied in loading it up with big wooden crates.

"Whatever could be in those crates?"

Lucy-Ann wondered.

Philip shrugged. All he was concerned about was finding and rescuing Bill. He took Lucy-Ann's hand and helped her up the hill.

When they reached the top they found Jack and Dinah looking up at a tall security fence. On the other side of it, a flock of sheep were grazing. It seemed that part of Perez's estates served as a sheep farm, although none of them had ever seen such elaborate security in any sort of farm before. A sign on the fence was painted with a skull and crossbones and said "Keep out!"

"Now what do we do?" asked Lucy-Ann.

"We climb over it, stupid!" said Philip and walked forwards. Dinah reached out and held him back.

"Wait!" she said.

She bent down and picked up a stick and held it up to the fence. There was an ominous crackling noise and they all watched on, horrified, as the stick burnt away to a cinder.

"That could have been you, Philip!" Jack said. "The fence is electrified! Now how do we get in?"

CHAPTER SEVENTEEN

"Stop this! I'm an innocent ornithologist!" Tipperlong protested as he was led into the tank room with his hands tied behind his back. "This is an outrage!"

Perez looked up briefly as Bruce dragged Tipperlong into the room. He was unwrapping a magnificent piece of sculpture from an oilskin and was more concerned about this than about the insignificant little man who'd just been brought to him.

"Please, take a chair," he said.

"What is the meaning of this?" shouted Tipperlong. "I demand an explanation! I am an internationally acclaimed ornithologist!"

"I, too, have an international reputation," answered Perez mildly. He gestured to his men to place Tipperlong in a chair next to Bill.

Bill was slumped on the floor against the shark tank, also with his hands tied behind his back. There was an exhausted expression on his face and the dark circles under his eyes showed that he hadn't slept much the previous night. He had another cut on his forehead where one of Perez's thugs had struck him in an effort to beat some information out of him.

Tipperlong continued to protest, until Bruce waved a revolver menacingly in his face. He looked at Bill, who nodded a brief hello, and he wondered where he had seen the face before. Finally it dawned on him. Bill had been connected with those blasted kids, he realised.

Bill, however, was much more interested in Perez. Together with some of his assistants the South American was wrapping a wide variety of objects in bubble-wrap. There were fine-looking vases from the Ming dynasty in China; heavy silver candlesticks encrusted with rubies and emeralds; fine necklaces; and ancient Maori masks and carvings. All of them were works of art, and together they were worth a small fortune.

After Perez had wrapped each item up in its protective bubble-wrap, he placed them in a small crate. The way he handled them was delicate, loving, even, as well it should be, Bill thought. He knew that even the smallest of those works of art would bring in millions of dollars if they were sold to Perez's contacts on the black market.

But how was Perez going to smuggle the crates past customs? Bill had to know. Then he watched as Perez's henchmen placed freshly-caught fish and ice on top of the bubble-wrapped objects. Finally the crates were closed shut, a label reading "Keep chilled" pasted on the side, and they were carried out to the waiting *Espadon*.

Bill had to admire Perez's ingenuity. If he was stopped at Customs and any of the crates were opened, then the Customs Officers would just see the packed fish, and not the priceless treasures they concealed.

Perez turned and smiled at Bill. "Who says that crime doesn't pay?" he asked smugly.

"You'll never win, Perez," Bill retorted.

"Aha, but I *am* winning, Mister Cunningham," Perez pointed out. "Now, have you reconsidered? Are you prepared to tell me how much your organisation knows about me?"

"You'll never get anything out of me, Perez!" Bill said defiantly.

"I will leave you five more minutes to reconsider," Perez said. "And then. . . well, I rather think it will be feeding time, don't you?" He glanced at the shark in the nearby tank.

Perez left the room to supervise the loading of the *Espadon*, and told Davey to keep a watchful eye on the two men. When he had gone, Tipperlong turned to Bill.

"'Feeding time'?" he asked nervously. "What did he mean?"

Bill looked over at the killer shark swimming in its tank: "Believe me, Mister

Tipperlong," he said grimly, "you really do not want to know!"

Lucy-Ann looked unconvinced as Philip and Jack led her to the electrified fence. Each of the two boys was holding a long branch in his hands. On the other side of the fence the sheep were watching in interest. Lucy-Ann glanced over to them. They didn't look particularly appreciative of the boys' hare-brained scheme either, she decided.

"Are you sure this is going to work?" she asked doubtfully.

"Of course it is!" Jack said confidently. "Trust us."

"Jack and I will hold the fence open with these two branches while you crawl through," Philip explained to her once more.

Lucy-Ann took a deep breath. "Well, here goes," she said, and went down on her hands and knees.

The boys wedged the branches under the wire and lifted, making a space wide enough for Lucy-Ann to crawl through without coming into contact with the fence itself.

The second they did so, a klaxon sounded throughout the grounds. Not only was the fence booby-trapped, it was alarmed too!

"Come on, Lucy-Ann! Crawl through!" said Jack.

Lucy-Ann did as she was told and was followed by Dinah and Jack. Philip then pushed the two branches through the holes in the fence and Dinah and Jack lifted open the wire for him as well.

They staggered to their feet and looked round. The klaxon had stopped now but they knew that the place would be swarming with guards any second now.

"We've got to hide!" Dinah said and looked round.

"But where?" Lucy-Ann asked. They were out in open ground and there was nowhere they could run to.

"We dig a hole?" Jack suggested, not very helpfully.

Philip looked at the flock of sheep grazing peacefully in the field, unconcerned by the fact that he and the others would soon be Perez's prisoners. A smile crossed his face.

"I think I've got an idea," he told them.

CHAPTER EIGHTEEN

Moments later, Bruce and a vicious-looking guard entered the field, their guns at the ready. They looked around. There was no sign of any intruder, only the flock of sheep happily munching away at the grass. They lowered their guns.

"One of the sheep must have brushed against the fence," Bruce said and replaced his gun in the holster at his side. "It looks like they got away with it this time."

"Shame," his colleague joked, as they walked back together to the main building. "I was looking forward to a roast lamb supper tonight."

As soon as they had gone, Philip, Jack, Dinah and Lucy-Ann emerged from their hiding place in the middle of the flock of sheep. Lucy-Ann gave one of the sheep a pat on the head by way of thanks for concealing them. The sheep baa-ed indifferently and returned to her grazing.

"Now to rescue Bill!" Philip said.

Keeping as well out of sight as possible, Philip, Jack, Dinah and Lucy-Ann squeezed through a hole in the wall of the main building of Perez's headquarters. As they did so, they narrowly missed running straight into Perez himself, who was returning from the *Espadon*. They dived behind a pile of equipment and watched as he entered the building.

"Who's that?" Lucy-Ann asked.

"A nasty piece of work, that's for sure," Philip replied.

"Do you think he's holding Bill prisoner?" asked Dinah.

"Well, there's only one way to find out, isn't there?" Jack said. Philip moved towards the back of the building Perez had just entered, but Dinah stopped him.

"No," she said. "It's my turn."

She tiptoed out from behind the equipment and crossed the yard towards the door Perez had gone through. She opened it and was about to go through it when she heard voices coming towards her. She ran back to the others and ducked down just in time to escape Perez's notice as he stepped back into the yard.

"Bring the prisoners here," Perez said.

Bruce came through the door, bringing Bill and Tipperlong and followed by Davey and another guard. They forced the prisoners to their knees. Perez smiled unpleasantly.

"Now, gentlemen, have you come to a decision?" he said.

"I don't know anything!" Tipperlong insisted. "I'm not with him, I told you! Please don't hit me again!"

Perez turned to Bill. "And what is your decision, Mister Cunningham?" he asked.

"I've nothing to say to you, Perez," Bill said. "My men are onto you."

"Really?" said Perez. Bill was bluffing and he knew it. "I don't hear the sound of the cavalry rushing to your rescue," he mocked.

"They'll be here," Bill said, as confidently as he was able.

"Unfortunately for you, they will be here too late," Perez said dismissively. He turned to Bruce. "Is your little playmate ready?" he asked.

"Sharks are just eating machines," Bruce said and rubbed his hands gleefully. "They're always ready for some tucker."

"No! No!" whimpered Tipperlong as he felt his knees knocking together with fear. "Please don't feed me to the sharks! I'll tell you anything you want to know."

"Aha, but you have just told me that you don't know anything," Bruce said with a smile.

"Now, Cunningham, I'm a fair man," Perez said. "I'll give you five more minutes to consider your options."

"You'll never get anything from me," Bill said flatly.

"As you wish," Perez said and clicked his fingers at one of the guards to follow him. "I shall be waiting for your decision in my office down the corridor."

Davey and the guard forced Bill and Tipperlong onto the metal gantry overlooking the shark tank. The shark circled in the water, sensing its supper.

Tipperlong could hardly stand now, so consumed with fright was he. Even Bill was looking worried: he really couldn't see any way out of this one.

Jack turned to the others in horror. "They're going to feed Bill to the sharks!" he told them. "We've only got another five minutes! We've got to do something – and fast!"

CHAPTER NINETEEN

Outside the back room, Philip and Jack checked and synchronised their watches. One second out in their timing and Bill and Tipperlong would be sharkmeat.

Philip was holding a long stick which he'd found dumped in the yard. It wasn't ideal for what he had in mind but it would have to serve. He just hoped that the girls would perform their part of the operation perfectly. It all depended on them now.

Next door to the back room, Perez was at his desk examining some papers when he heard a noise in the corridor outside. Or rather not a noise – a song.

"Me huri au ki Te Awarua o Porirua," sang Lucy-Ann, who together with Dinah had managed to sneak into the

corridor through an open window.

Perez raced over to the door to his office and opened it just in time to see Dinah and Lucy-Ann rushing off down the corridor.

"After them!" he cried to his guard, and the guard ran out of the room in pursuit. Perez went back to his desk and pressed a button. Alarm bells started to ring all over the complex.

Up the stairs by the gantry Bruce also ran off, leaving only Davey and one guard and, of course, Bill and Tipperlong. Philip and Jack climbed up the steps and plotted. Philip hid while Jack sauntered casually over to Bill and the guards.

"Excuse me, please, I'm lost," he said to Davey. "Can you help me?" He sounded for all the world like a little boy who had strayed from his parents at a fairground.

"Jack!" Bill couldn't believe his eyes.

Neither for that matter could Davey. He stared in disbelief at Jack for a second, and made to grab him.

"Jack! Run!" cried Bill.

Jack had the advantage of surprise and he easily evaded the burly man. He ran down the steps but Davey whipped the revolver out of his holster. He was about to fire when Philip leapt out of his hiding place and knocked the revolver out of Davey's hand with his stick. It clattered to the ground, just out of his reach.

Davey growled with anger and turned on Philip. Then he backed away as Philip approached him, holding his stick in front of him like a taiaha. Philip waved the stick expertly in the air, swiping at the man and making him duck.

Up on the gantry, the remaining guard was momentarily distracted, uncertain whether to stay up there or climb down to help his colleague. Bill noticed the hesitation and lunged against him. Taken by surprise, the guard fell from the gantry, straight into the shark tank!

Tipperlong looked down in horror at the tank. The water below seethed and slowly turned a horrible shade of red as the shark feasted on its long-awaited meal.

"Don't just stand there!" Bill commanded. "Turn round and untie me!"

Down below, Davey had grabbed a stick of his own and, with an angry shout, brought the stick crashing down upon Philip's head. Philip ducked just in the nick of time, and with an upward sweep of his makeshift taiaha knocked the weapon out of Davey's hands.

Davey backed away again towards the closed door which led into the corridor. Suddenly he dropped to his knees and picked up the revolver which Philip had knocked out of his hands before. He smiled as he pointed the gun at Philip and Jack.

"Now I've got you," he said, and looked up as Bill and Tipperlong, their hands now untied, ran down the steps. "And you two can stop where you are as well!" he snarled.

Suddenly the door burst open and Dinah and Lucy-Ann hurtled outside. Davey was knocked sideways, and fell to the floor, cracking his head and losing consciousness for vital seconds. Bill held the door closed and locked it quickly.

They weren't free yet, Bill realised.

"Well done, kids," he congratulated them. "We've got to think fast. This door won't hold long. Where are you anchored?"

Philip told them where they had moored Tipperlong's boat.

"Right, I'm going to get into a wet suit and cause a diversion," Bill told them. "Meet me at the point on the south side of the island in ten minutes."

Philip, Jack, Dinah and Lucy-Ann, along with Tipperlong, hurried back to the motorboat. When they reached the shore, Kiki squawked a welcome.

"Pieces of eight!" she said loudly, until Jack hushed her. They didn't want her attracting the attention of any guards!

"What if we can't pick Mr Cunningham up?" asked Tipperlong as he started up his boat and steered her to the small promontory where Bill had said he'd meet up with them.

"We just have to, that's all," Dinah said firmly.

Perez and Bruce broke down the door to the yard to find Davey sprawled out on the ground. Seeing that Bill and the others had escaped, Perez ran down to the jetty. He could see the *Lucky Star* a little way out to sea. One of the guards lay unconscious nearby. It was clear that Bill had overpowered him and commandeered the boat.

"Come on! Come on!" he ordered the guards who had followed him. "They're getting away!"

They boarded the *Espadon* and set off in hot pursuit, chopping through the waves as fast as they could. It was a much faster craft than the *Lucky Star*, and they caught up within minutes. They drew level and prepared to board.

"Blast him!" said Perez.

Bruce could now see what the matter was. There was no one on board. The wheel had been immobilised with a length of rope, and the steering had been put on automatic!

"We'll find them!" Perez swore. "And when we do, we shoot – to kill!"

his wetsuit pulled to this waist
Tipperlong grinned. Yes," comeone said
"Have you got enough for all of us," he

CHAPTER TWENTY

Tipperlong drew his boat up to where Bill had arranged to meet them, just off a rocky point. While the older man stayed at the wheel, the children and Kiki peered over the stern. Where was Bill? It was much more than ten minutes, and they were all getting worried.

Bill surfaced out of the water wearing a wet suit, snorkel and flippers.

"There he is!" cried Philip, and they all helped him aboard.

"Worked like a charm," said Bill.

"Have we lost them?" asked Philip, scanning the sea for a sight of the *Espadon*.

"Well, they're headed north, anyway, following a boat with nobody on it! And we're going home. South, Mr

Tipperlong," he called. "Due South."

Tipperlong grinned and saluted. He started up the engine and turned the boat.

Suddenly Lucy-Ann spotted something.

"Look! Look!" she cried. Everyone turned round. Coming around the point was the *Espadon*! They hadn't lost Perez after all!

Tipperlong frowned because his boat was slowing down. He checked the fuel gauge and found his worst fears realised: it was reading empty.

Jack peered at the approaching craft through his binoculars. Perez, Bruce and Davey had their guns out and ready. It was only a matter of time before they caught up with them!

"Quick, find something we can defend ourselves with!" Bill ordered and everyone dashed below deck, ransacking the cupboards for anything which could be of use.

"What are we looking for, Uncle Bill?" Lucy-Ann asked.

"Anything that might help, Lucy-Ann," he said, although in truth he didn't know what could save them now.

"Will this do?" asked Philip, producing a harpoon gun.

"Well, it's a good try," Bill said, "but I doubt it'll stop Perez for long."

Their search was fruitless and they returned on deck. Tipperlong handed the wheel over to Philip.

"A distress flare! A distress flare! I've seen a distress flare somewhere!" He hurried off to see if he could find it.

It took him several seconds – valuable seconds, as the *Espadon* drew closer and closer – but he finally found a cardboard box with the distress flare in it, and held it aloft. He took his lighter from out of his pocket, and was just about to light it when Dinah screamed. She pointed out the writing on the tube.

"It's dynamite!" she said.

Tipperlong dropped the tube in panic, and Bill snatched it up again. Already an idea was forming in his mind.

"Philip, give me your penknife," he

rapped out. Then he opened the tube at one end, carefully pouring the gunpowder out of the tube before resealing it. Tipperlong watched on, puzzled; he hadn't the faintest idea what Bill was up to.

"What are you doing?" he asked. "It won't blow up now there's no gunpowder inside."

Bill grinned. "I know that, Horace," he said. "But Perez and his friends don't!"

Then he said, "Jack, pass me the harpoon gun, please."

The *Espadon* was practically on top of them now. The children watched on, as mystified as Mr Tipperlong, as Bill attached the useless flare to the end of the harpoon. He took Tipperlong's lighter and lit the fuse. He raced up on deck to where he could see the Espadon, now drawing alongside with Perez, Bruce and two other guards lined up with their guns at the ready.

Bill fired the harpoon, smoking flare and all, towards the *Espadon*. It landed on the deck of the *Espadon* with a *thunk!* and

Perez, Bruce, Davey and the guard looked on in horror at the smoking stick of explosive.

"Jump!" Bruce screamed out. He dropped his gun on the deck and dived into the sea. Perez and Davey needed no further encouragement and followed his example, swimming frantically as fast as they could away from the boat before the expected explosion.

Bill jumped neatly over from Tipperlong's boat to the *Espadon*. He picked up one of the discarded revolvers, as well as the stick of dynamite. As the children, Kiki and Tipperlong came over to join him, he looked over the side of the boat and called after Perez.

Perez turned in the water to see Bill aiming a gun at him and his two henchmen. Bill waved the smoking stick of dynamite in the air.

"Bang," he said simply, and tossed the dynamite into the water. It was then that Perez realised that he'd been fooled and, as Philip went to radio the coastguard, the South American also knew that his days of smuggling and killing and cheating were finally over.

EPILOGUE

The *Espadon* glided into harbour like a stately galleon, accompanied on the starboard and port side by two other boats. Perez and his men were now in the safe hands of the police.

Philip, Jack, Dinah and Lucy-Ann peered over the side of the cruiser as it docked. Waiting for them at the harbour were several more policemen – and Alison and Dennis.

"Mum! Mum!" called out Dinah. "You wouldn't believe what an adventure we've had!"

Alison waved back at them delightedly. For the past few days she'd been worried sick when she'd heard nothing from them. She'd called Bill's mobile phone several times and when there had been no answer her imagination had been working overtime, imagining all kinds of terrible things which could have happened to them.

"We were chased by art thieves," Lucy-Ann told her, as she ran ashore to hug Alison.

"But we fooled them with dynamite!" added Jack, coming up to join them.

"Only it wasn't dynamite after all!" put in Philip.

All this was too much for Alison to take in at one go. "Hang on!" she said.

"Start at the beginning!" Dinah told them. "Start at the beginning!"

"We were all alone on this deserted island in this big storm," Lucy-Ann began.

"Except it wasn't deserted, 'cos then we met Te Araki," said Philip.

"And then we followed the art thieves to their island," said Jack.

Alison looked up at Bill, who was coming to join them after he had seen that Perez, Bruce and Davey were in the capable hands of Dennis and the New

Zealand police. They shared a look which seemed to say: *Kids! What can you do with them! You certainly can't stop them from having adventures!*

"And we haven't eaten anything but beans for days!" said Lucy-Ann, which was a slight exaggeration to say the least, but it still produced the desired effect.

"You poor things!" Alison said, and ruffled Lucy-Ann's blonde hair sympathetically. "Come and have something to eat and you can tell me all about it."

"That's a great idea!" Dinah agreed enthusiastically.

"There's a wonderful new restaurant I've found on the harbour," Alison told them. "It does the most marvellous shark steaks."

Everyone, including Bill, groaned.

"What did I say?" asked Alison.

"Thanks, Aunt Allie," said Jack with a grin, "but I think we've all had enough of sharks to last us a lifetime!"

The
Enid Blyton™
Adventure Series

All eight screenplay novelisations from the Channel 5 series are available from bookshops or, to order direct from the publishers, just make a list of the titles you want and send it with your name and address to:

Dept 6,
HarperCollins*Publishers* Ltd,
Westerhill Road,
Bishopbriggs,
Glasgow G64 2QT

Please enclose a cheque or postal order to the value of the cover price (currently £3.50) plus:

UK and BFPO: Add £1 for the first book, and 25p per copy for each additional book ordered.

Overseas and Eire: Add £2.95 service charge. Books will be sent by surface mail, but quotes for airmail dispatch will be given on request.

A 24-hour telephone ordering service is available to Visa and Access card holders on 0141-772 2281.